Richard D. Besecker

Rick Besecker was raised in the magnificent Colorado Cochetopa/La Garita Wilderness area. With life on a rustic guest ranch, one is required to contribute to the necessities for daily survival; and, at an uncommon youthful age. At five years old there was water to be hauled in galvanized buckets from the spring house, firewood to be carried from the woodshed, and kerosene lamps that needed to be filled each day. By seven, Rick was introduced to the udder end of a Jersey, and was now proficient with splitting firewood, and expected to operate a John Deere with a mower and buck rake. There was no distraction from hard work or, for that matter, hard play. Without electricity, entertainment was self-initiated and would encompass shooting prairie dogs, playing cowboys and Indians on horseback, fly fishing, hunting for Native American artifacts, and conducting Jeep tours in the back country. He shot his first deer at age 12 and his first bear at 13. And, to impress upon the man child the spiritual concept related to harvesting wild game, he was required to field dress and process the reward.

School was a 100-mile traverse each day. Although Rick was uncomfortable with the social concept of the classroom, he was ruler of the weekends and most classmates were eager to experience the "Old West" on the Quarter-Circle Circle Ranch.

Stardust Christmas

By Richard D. Besecker

Devereux
Publishing

Devereux Publishing
159 North Road
Gunnison, CO 81230

Dedicated to the memory of Margaret Mary Besecker and her granddaughter, Mariah Gene Besecker-Green

Stardust Christmas

Stardust Night

Lee ran his fingers along the full distance of the freshly chromed fin; the very contours of which made her a classic from the beginning. Now, more than ever, Detroit's best seemed to become increasingly enhanced with the distinction that this inanimate object held over late model cars. She was a 1957 Bel Air Hardtop - the chariot of which drew transportation and romance together. Midsummer night drag races, moonlit kisses, small town cruising and all demonstrations of passionate romance, if done correctly, were embraced in the front cushion of a '57 Chevy.

"Stardust," Lee announced as he fervently christened the metal-flaked metallic, starlit pearl, time machine. There were five coats of lacquer over a brilliant ultra-white finish which gave an incredible depth to her appearance. She was obviously solid. A tangible mass of perfection in every conceivable way from the seductive breast shaped front bumper to the fin ends of her stern. Every imaginable detail had been thought through and only the absolute finest materials had been selected for classic enhancement. She was complete, she was paid for and she belonged to Lee who was a rugged appearing 24-year-old man who focused on personal aspirations and not so much the consideration of others. As a result, the filling station employee's only real possession was a car which had been manufactured some six-plus decades ago.

Stardust had survived over 65 years of memories, 5 of which were spent in limbo due to restorations. Now she most definitely triumphed as the best in her class. The only problem was that the vehicle, as well as its master's attitude, had become antiquated: the car by age and the man by choice.

Lee embraced a simpler time when ills of machinery could be resolved through the application of baling wire, duct tape and imagination. This was when the phrase "metric measurement" was most definitely a foreign term and if your best girl left you for another man, you always had faith that your "wheels" would never let you down. Indeed, Lee Fairchild was born several decades too late. His taste for clothing, music, and his appreciation for fine machinery was in the era when Elvis Presley, the Everly Brothers and Buddy Holly were common household vernacular.

Suddenly, there was a shrill sound of a door buzzer which rudely interrupted quality time between man and "beast." As Lee opened the back door to the small paint-peeled drab dwelling otherwise known as *Jake's Gas and Repair Shop*, he would turn and glance one last time at the car of his dreams. Reflecting the pale blue fluorescent illumination of the alley light, she stood out as a fantasy in the fresh December snow.

Jake's Place

Lee made his way through the cramped disarray of new as well as old tires; the pillars of which reached so high as to nearly eclipse the already struggling luster of the single 60-watt bulb that gave its all to light the pit area of the garage. A young lady was standing in the doorway of the small business office which, with some imagination, doubled as a reception area. Her white down jacket was smudged around the sleeves and the pockets. Through elementary observation this was a garment of many miles. She wore pants that may have matched something out of grandma's closet eons ago, and the low-cut shoes she sported revealed that her delicate feet were without socks. Such an obvious oversight gave way to certain discomfort in the dead of winter. Her general attire gave the first impression that she was perhaps a transient living off the street. However, her penetrating green eyes and radiant smile gave an indication that there, under this wardrobe confusion, dwelt the possibilities of uncommon beauty which distracted Lee's attention from such drab clothing.

Sensing that it must be getting quite late, Lee glanced at the old antique Coca Cola clock which was hanging just a little off center above the doorframe behind the young lady. The slightly bent hands of the vintage timepiece indicated the approaching midnight hour, more or less, and thus past closing time, more or less, on this Christmas Eve.

"We're closed," Lee simply said.

"Please sir," The stranger implored with a desperate tone and with those mesmerizing but pleading eyes. "I was so relieved to see your light still on and the door was not locked, and nothing else is open."

Lee found himself somewhat amused, if not bewildered. After all, what would a person like this be doing seeking an apparent shopping outlet in a dump like this. And, at this late hour?

"We only sell gas and tires and some of those are marginal at best," he said as he pointed his thumb over his shoulder and in the general direction of the overabundant selection of new and used inventory.

She looked down at the glass case which safely guarded several partial boxes of the same kind of candy. Henry Ford was once heard to have said that it did not matter which kind of car you owned, or even the color, so long as it was a black Ford. When it came to candy, old man Jake maintained the same approach to his favorite selection and subsequent display of Snickers caramel and chocolate bars.

With obvious apprehension, the shivering young lady raised her arm which revealed a delicate hand clad only in a fingerless glove. Pointing in the direction of the candy she asked with modest apprehension, "How much?"

"The candy bars are a dollar fifty each," Lee impatiently responded.

With some difficulty, she slowly lifted a tattered and darned sock and, adorning a somewhat worried smile, she began to dump the contents onto the glass countertop. Without warning, it would seem that hundreds of pennies, some nickels and a few dimes began to roll in as many directions all at once. Quickly reacting with somewhat disgust, Fairchild fenced off the runaway coins best that he could.

"I hope I have enough money for two candy bars each!" she exclaimed.

"And how many would that be?" Lee inquired with somewhat an impatient tone to his voice.

"Six. But I am not sure that I have enough money."

It became apparent to the gas station employee that the real tragedy was not the young lady's personal destitution, but that of a combined nature involving perhaps, a few more lonesome souls. Lee pushed the apparent sole possessions of the would-be midnight shopper back across the glass surface in a non-accepting manner which invoked an instant and all-consuming terror expressed on the young lady's lovely face. Sensing the unnecessary distress, Lee put his hand up as to gesture a halt to such tension and he smiled.

"Here," he said as he reached for a half-filled box of the neatly wrapped chocolate delights. "There should be about a dozen or so."

"Oh sir," she said, appearing stunned, but hopeful. "I can't possibly accept these. They are to be gifts *from* me, not *to* me."

Although the self-relying Lee did not entirely understand what the big deal was, he sensed that this miniscule moment was apparently paramount to the young lady and, if it would get her on her way a contribution would surely be in order.

"Jake, the owner of this place, told me the other day to throw these boxes out 'cause they were getting too old for resale," the white fib escaped Lee's lips. "So really, you would be doing me a tremendous favor. Besides, what else are you going to do?"

With tears welling up in her eyes, she scooped up the change and returned it to the old gray sock, placed it in the box on top of her newly acquired treasures, and then placed the bundle under her left arm.

"Thank you so much! My name is Sheila," the pretty young lady said as she extended the fragile, lilywhite hand and at the same time a lone tear began to streak down her attractive cheek.

As Lee accepted her gesture, he could feel that her fingers were still ice cold. Their eyes met for just a brief but tantalizing moment and, with a slight hint of a smile, she withdrew her limb.

"Lee... Leland Fairchild," he tried to respond as perhaps James Bond would.

"I must get back before the little ones miss me too much." Sheila paused and then advanced towards the door. "God bless you, Mr. Fairchild. And I hope that the rest of your night is extraordinary." Then, with a sincere "Merry Christmas," she lit out with great haste.

18 Degrees Below Zero

Lee locked the door behind the young lady and watched as she shuffled off into the bitter cold. He slowly reached down in his front pocket until he could feel crumpled bills and withdrew some money. Pulling a 20-dollar bill from the unorganized bundle, he hit the release bar on the antique cash register and simultaneously looked out of the frosted front window of the store. His eyes focused on the bank clock beyond the scurrying girl and with sudden alarm felt a gripping concern. The temperature reading was -18 degrees! How far did she have to go?

Lee tried to imagine the kind of place where she might live. The only run-down shack he could think of in this part of town was the place where he worked. And the sole reason the City of Gunnison had not condemned the garage was because it was owned by his 107-year-old great, great grandfather, Jake Fairchild, who happened to be the oldest citizen in the entire county, maybe even the state.

Lee quickly turned the tattered and smudged open/closed sign around to closed, twisted the dead bolt of the front door, and rushed through the cluttered maze in the garage area. As he stepped through the rear exit of the business, the cold was most sobering. Feeling increasingly frustrated, he fumbled with the hasp and large lock securing the rickety back door. It was ironic that old man Jake Fairchild thought it necessary to place a 60-dollar padlock on such a likeness. Finally, he felt the steel loop of the frosted lock slide into place and latch.

Lee wondered where the poor girl named Sheila was by now, and if she was alright. He quickly unplugged the block heater and climbed into his classic automobile. A growing sense of urgency was building as he turned the key to engage the ignition switch. Although the engine block was relatively warm, the heavy horses protested the rude awakening from their frozen midnight slumber. Finally, the engine turned, coughed and fired to a hesitant start. Lee's impatience was growing as he knew that it would take time for the life extending oil to reach acceptable warmth to function as intended. Pushed with panic, he gave in to the pressure, blurted out an apology to his classic car, and pushed the shifter into first.

With frantic persuasion, he steered his machine to the right and then down the main avenue. Main Street was completely vacant of traffic, even parked cars. Thousands of blinking Christmas lights announced the approach of the Christians' valued day, but no one was present to appreciate the beauty other than Lee and, perhaps, the desperate soul for which he was searching.

After a few aimless minutes, an uncomfortable feeling persuaded Lee to turn down County Road 13, otherwise known as Slaughterhouse Road. By the pale-yellow illumination of his headlights, the old rusted steel truss that supported the ever-aging Slaughterhouse Bridge gave Lee shivers which raced up his spine as he realized that the outdated structure sustained all the visual appeal of a medieval drawbridge on a dark path to a satanic castle. Without truly understanding why, he was persuaded through the depths of the darkness as he drove on. He had not been this way for several years, and he could not figure out why he felt the irresistible urge to do so now. The old slaughterhouse, located at the end of a two-mile drive, had burned down over 80 years ago and now served only to attract junior voyagers on warm summer day explorations. To Lee's knowledge, nothing else existed on this eerie, lonesome path but the footprints in the snow urged him on.

I Can't Feel My Fingers

With curiosity, Lee's eyes focused on an unidentifiable object at a distance down the road. As he approached, Lee braked to a halt. He felt his heart sink as his car's headlight revealed Sheila was on her hands and knees attempting to pick up the money and candy bars that she had apparently dropped. Her frozen fingers were too numb to feel, and every grasp was in vain.

Lee stepped out of the automobile into the once again sobering cold of the midnight air. With tears streaming down her face, she raised her hands. It was with obvious exasperation she exclaimed, "They hurt so much, yet I can't feel to touch! It doesn't make sense!"

With deliberate care Lee slowly lifted the young lady to her feet and escorted her to the safety of the still warming car. With Lee's instructions, Sheila placed her freezing hands under her modest blouse and next to her tummy in order to accelerate the warmth to her fingers. Lee then returned to retrieve the young damsel's belongings.

After accomplishing the task, the two just sat for several minutes and talked while the young girl regained the feeling in her extremities. The heater was finally blowing warm air and Sheila appeared to be feeling much better. Now, once again, she voiced her concern about her absence from the children, so Lee followed her directions down Slaughterhouse Road. As they drove along, Lee became privy to the circumstances that the young lady had to endure. Sheila said that she never really knew her father all that well as he was gone most of the time. Then, he had left for good while her mother was still pregnant with the youngest sibling. He was never to be heard from again. Her mother raised Sheila, her two younger sisters, and their youngest sibling, a brother, the best that she could, but ended up dying last summer.

Sheila did not say how she died, and with respectful reverence Lee did not ask. Sheila went on to say that on the very day they laid their mother to rest they were asked to leave their apartment as the landlord feared that they would not be able to maintain the rent.

A legal document left by her mother instructed that 60 acres, otherwise known as The Old Slaughterhouse Ruins, be bequeathed unto her, so that was where she and her siblings would embrace their destiny. She had never been to Colorado, but the brave 18-year-old resigned herself to be the children's ward and began the long journey to colorful Colorado from New Jersey.

As they rounded the last bend in the narrow road, Lee saw a pale glimmer of a lamplight in the window of a makeshift shack. He learned that Sheila had spent the last of her meager inheritance on materials and had contracted labor to build the slab-sided dwelling that she and the kids now knew as home. It may be small, but Lee could tell it was a castle in what was left of the hearts of the insolvent family. As they drove closer, Lee could see smoke curling upward from the stove pipe and a silhouette of a small person's head in the window. Sheila smiled with pride.

"That's three-year-old Jasmine," she said. "She may be a little rascal at times, but she is my tough little trooper. Nothing much gets her down unless I'm late getting home. Then she worries."

Then there was a second silhouette. "That's Isabelle. She is seven and what a magnificent little princess." And then, a third "bump" as two-year-old Jordan attempted to see out the window as well. Finally, Isabelle lifted the tyke up so he could peer out too.

Sheila went on, "And Jordan gets into everything" A frown overtook the pretty face as she went on, "He even burnt his hand on the heating stove a week ago and he has not gotten close to that again."

"Are you alright?" Lee inquired with still mounting concern.

"Yes. And thank you so much for rescuing me - twice." Looking at her hands and then at Lee, she broke out in an alluring smile, and with a sudden and deliberate motion leaned over and before Lee knew it, he felt her soft lips brush his cheek.

"Nice car," she simply said as she stepped back into the elements and then closed the door. With haste, Lee opened his door and stepped out but, before he could catch her attention, Sheila ran inside the little shack. Lee slowly raised his hand and gave a feeble motion of farewell that Sheila would not see. However, the gesture was not entirely in vain as the three little people silhouetted in the window waved back.

After a twelve-hour shift at the pumps earlier that day, Lee had once anticipated trudging his exhausted, weary bones to his single room apartment in Ma's boarding house and watching his small television until Ma Kettle, as she was affectionately referred to, shut him down. It seemed that the old lady had "twenty-twenty" hearing. His mind was racing however, and instead of being tired, he felt somehow, someway motivated—even exhilarated. It was a positive mixture of vibes stemming from the rescue of the damsel in actual distress and the soft brush of a kiss that he could not dismiss. And, the mixture of unexpected feelings was exciting. Lee somehow wanted it to not end - ever!

As he drove back through the once ominous skeletal over structure of the steel I-beam construction, the Slaughterhouse Bridge no longer seemed the large, rusty dragon which stood guard at the gateway to a forbidden land. Lee gazed in the rearview mirror. Nothing but darkness reflected back. Nevertheless, just beyond the depths of such darkness, a warm little cottage existed. And within that humble slab house was a magnificent young lady that Lee had once mistaken for a common transient.

Pulling the steering wheel abruptly to the right, the Chevy responded as Lee pushed the accelerator to the floor. At first, she fishtailed, and then her momentum matched the tire speed. As she caught hold, Lee could feel his back pushing hard into the seat. The roar from split pipes reverberated off the store fronts as Stardust raced down the main avenue. Through town he drove and then out on Gold Basin Road he sped. The ever-advancing rate of motion gave a whistling sound indicating that this was truly a fine automobile. After a swift couple of miles on a straightaway, Lee backed his foot off and the massive engine mellowed its mighty roar.

"What a great night and all you peasants are wasting it by sleeping it away," Lee thought to himself.

As he turned the radio on, he prepared to lie back a little and simply cruise and listen to memory sounds that matched the day when Stardust was first conceived. He thumped on the fuel gauge with his finger, which indicated a little less than a fourth of a tank, and waited for the old tube radio to warm up.

My Friends Call Me Nicky

"Yours truly, KEJJ, the Edge; 98.3 on your FM dial; your instant access to the best of golden age Rock 'n Roll," the jingle leaped across the airway and into Lee's four speakers with enthusiasm. "Goooooooooood morning, late night crawlers! This is Harv Rees telling you that some fluffy dude dressed in fire engine red and flying at low altitude has just been spotted by NORAD officials. And they say he is entering our hemisphere! Imagine that!"

Rees went on, "That reminds me, you sock stuff'n crazy citizens. They tell me that, according to the radar signatures, he is zigzagging around like a bloodhound apparently scouting out whoever is good and maybe not so good! Not that it matters to me! It has been my experience that he accelerates over my roof top for the past seven years in a row! What a punk. You would think he would at least give a token gesture and slow a bit on the fly by. Nevertheless, the so-called unidentified inbound object is on a final approach just outside of town," Harv said, maintaining his relentless dialog. "Anyone out there know Santa's wife's name? No, not Mrs. Claus! Don't be boring! We are talking first name, you silly Santa believers!" There was a pause for a minute before the crazy man blurted out, "Believe it or not it's *Sheila!*"

Sheila by Tommy Roe, to be exact! If you don't believe me just ask me!"

Suddenly the popular tune from 1962 pierced the airways. Lee felt compelled to stop in the middle of the county highway and gaze upward into the dark star-speckled heavens. He stepped outside, closed the door and again took in all the heavenly wonders that seemed to be exclusive to him, and maybe Harv. The sub-zero temperature could not counter the new-found warmth in Lee's heart. He seemed to be more alive than ever. He was not sure he could comprehend it all as he sang to the muffled lyrics coming from his car, *"Oh my little Sheila, sweet Little Sheila- her name drives me insane..."*

Lee's deep thoughts were interrupted by the brilliance of a large falling sphere as it streaked across the endless sky in a semi horizontal but declining plane. He immediately began to concentrate on a wish of all wishes. Not that he believed in such idiotic notions, but somehow, he was compelled. After all, by popular belief, this was the night for miracles if ever there were such things.

Lee's concentration was short lived as he realized that the meteor had struck just a short distance down the road and off to the east.

"Far out," Lee found himself announcing out loud. He climbed into Stardust with purpose and kicked in the afterburners. Once again, the car fishtailed, gripped, and accelerated down the vacant road. The speedometer indicated close to 70 as he steered into a sharp, blind curve.

Lee was not prepared for what was around the bend. A very fat man was standing where Lee was intending to travel. Suddenly, Stardust slid first to the right and then to the left and, with brakes locked, spun a half orbit around the strange figure frozen with fear in the center of the blacktop. It seemed as though the large man had a protective force field, for there was not so much as a scratch on him. The car came to rest, still on its wheels, with the full beams shining on such a peculiar looking obstacle.

With a great belly laugh, the fat figure of a man passed one hand closely by the other and gave a vigorous kick with his right boot. "Sweet Jesus, that was close!" He understated the obvious. "And a fine piece of driving, I might add. Where did you learn to handle a machine like that?"

"What happened? I had my eyes shut!" Lee retorted with a tone of sarcasm as he climbed out of his ride and tugged at the seat portion of his Carhartt britches. He then redirected his attention to the rather overstuffed fellow who continued to be amused at the close call.

Lee projected himself in a brisk voice, "Try'n out to be a rather large speed bump?"

Laughing even harder now, the stranger was barely able to answer. "Didn't expect to see travelers this time of night, and I guess I was just deep in thought about things," the alien responded.

Appreciating his response, but still feeling a bit pushed by the inconsiderate pedestrian, Lee inquired, "What are you doing out here in the boonies? Where's your car?"

"Had some transportation problems, you might say," the stranger said as he pointed east of the roadway. Looking in the direction of which the fat fellow was pointing, Lee could see footprints through the freshly drifted snow. The markings led down the bank and onto the highway. Next to the bank was a large sack, which Lee assumed had this man's personal belongings within. Knowing of no roads in the direction from where he had apparently come and puzzled with the prospects of transportation in three feet of snow, Lee turned his attentions back to the stranger.

"What in the world were you doing?" Lee paused while peering at the illumination button on his digital watch, "...and at one o'clock in the morning?" As Lee carefully surveyed the strange man, he noticed that he was covered head to toe in soot. What once must have been a pair of shiny boots with silver buckles were now only scuffed remnants of such.

"You might say I crashed and burned," the strange fellow chuckled.

"You were in an aircraft?" Lee's suspicions were growing.

"I like to think of it more like a starship. You see, I have just one more town and then I head home; got to feeling a little bit too frisky and took her up too high."

"What in the heck are you talking about?" Lee demanded.

"I'm talk'n near space travel, boy!" The character responded as he slapped his hands together and then veered one hand off pointing it towards the sky. "I'm talking about scratching your head on the cosmos and reentering the atmosphere with your hair on fire; there is nothing like it!" He then tugged at his rather lengthy beard and went on, "burnt hair really stinks though, doesn't it?"

At that very moment, the pungent odor reached Lee's nostrils as though the mere suggestion had heightened his sense of smell. He noticed the fuzzy ball which was located at the end of the stranger's stocking cap was actually smoking! This man, whoever he was, was actually on fire! What worried Lee the most was the fact that he seemed to be enjoying it.

"When I was young, and that was a while ago, mind ya," he interrupted Lee's observations, "I helped brand cattle a couple of times, and I never *could* get used to that aroma."

"Who are you and what are you doing here?" Lee interrupted.

"Placing his hands on his hips and then looking off to one side in apparent disgust at himself, he gave a deep sigh. "Where are my manners? My friends get a kick outta call'n me Nicky," and he extended a chubby paw in Lee's direction.

Thinking that "Nicky" must have recently embraced the spirits, Lee reluctantly gripped the appendage that evidently belonged to a drunken, but joyful illusionist. He had never, to his recollection, ever met such a mentally challenged person before, but he was for sure in the presence of one now.

"Wow!" Nicky shrieked without warning causing Lee to stagger back with a start. "A '57 Bel Air, two-door, hardtop!" he exclaimed as he walked past Lee and stood in front of Lee's car. His arms were open, as if to embrace the entire inanimate object.

"Can I hitch a ride?" Nicky inquired with exuberance.

"Not without a damage deposit!" Lee thought to himself. Not only was it obvious that the man was not well from a psychological perspective, but he was still smoldering for heaven's sake!

Placing an ear close to the hood, Nicky began to grin as though he had just discovered a prize in a Cracker Jack box. "This thing ain't exactly stock, is it?" Without waiting for Lee's reply, he went on, "You're push'n a pre '67 Corvette 327, with a three-quarter cam and solid lifters; must be close to 375 horses pinned up in there. Maybe even 400 plus, at sea level. You can tell them horses are just chomp'n at the bit."

　　　Lee had his mouth open with an expression of total amazement on his face. Nicky took one look at Lee and began to belly roar once again.

Del Got It Right the First Time!

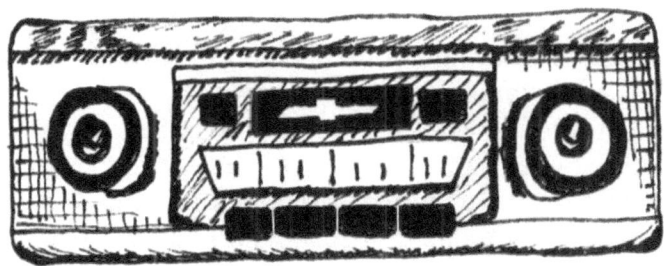

Perhaps it was the code of the Old West that specified that you never abandoned a man in the dead of winter, no matter how disengaged from reality he might be. Perhaps it was that "Nicky" so closely identified with Lee's passion for fine machinery. Whatever it was, it had taken hold. Before Lee knew it, the rather aromatic cuss and his rather large mystery sack were aboard the time machine and they were rapidly traveling back towards town.

They sped around one more curve and then into the one-mile straight away to the joyfully lit city. About this time, Del Shannon's all-time greatest hit "Runaway" began to reverberate from the speakers. On the very first note, Nicky got excited and, as he slapped his hands on his knees, exclaimed with great enthusiasm, "Alright! It don't get any better than this!"

Much to the young man's dismay, Nicky began to sing. There were only two problems with this. One, not only was he out of tune, but completely off key. Two, this was Del Shannon's masterpiece! This was the ultimate when it came to the mixture of voice and instrument. Nicky was destroying whatever shred of tolerance Lee could muster. The only reason the lad chose to put up with his presence in the first place was that Lee could not ignore the passion that the stranger seemed to have towards Stardust.

With as much tact as Lee could muster, Lee reached over and grabbed the charred coat sleeve of the untalented vocalist. "Don't do that!" Lee ordered through clenched teeth. "Del, got it right the first time."

"You are so right and I surely can take a hint," Nicky surrendered. "My wife says the same thing every time I try to serenade her. I sure don't sing all that well, but I sure do like trying. The only time I really sing well is when I am by myself, like when I am taking a shower, and then I can bring down the house. I wonder why that is? When I get out in public, it just won't come together. Sometime you will have to listen to me when I am all soaped up and alone."

All Lee could think of is, "Stop talking!" and, "No thanks!"

As much as Lee supported the notion of a bath for the old fella, he was repulsed at the thought of seeing him take it. Anyway, Nicky was so joyful about the whole thing that Lee could not help but appreciate his attitude, if not his lack of timing and harmonizing.

As they reached the edge of the city limits, the chubby fellow conveyed his appreciation for the lift and Lee dropped him off upon request. The bizarre man stood at his open-door chuckling for a moment.

"A finer ride I have never ridden," he said with a drawn-out sigh. Then, looking through the soft pale dome light and into the young man's eyes, he inquired with a serious overtone, "How old are you, son?" All of a sudden it seemed more personal. Lee did not know why, but he felt a little at risk by the question.

Caught off guard, Lee simply answered the question, "I'm 24. Why?"

The lad could hear Nicky pulling his large canvas bag across the tuck-n-roll ripples of the rear seat. "You're old enough to start think'n about settl'n down boy." He closed the door slightly harder than Lee approved, hoisted the overly filled sack to his shoulder, and looking expectantly at Lee who leaned over and rolled the window down. While leaning against the door's open window, he looked at Lee once again. "You sure can't do better than Sheila. Don't let her slip away," he instructed. Nicky then turned away and before the young man had a chance to say a word, the fat man seemed to vanish.

Lee reached across the seat to roll up the passenger side window before sitting up to scan the dimly lit street. He caught a brief glimpse of the overweight stranger three blocks away. The dude suddenly rounded the corner, dashed into an alley, and was out of sight again.

"Who is that plump fella?" Lee giggled to himself. He pushed down the accelerator in an attempt to chase the geriatric candidate How did he know about Sheila? How did he know Lee was even single? Furthermore, what business was it of his? Lee wanted answers!

For close to half an hour, Lee scanned the streets, looking in every alley and driveway. Finally, feeling fatigued, Lee decided to give up the ghost, and began the drive to his humble apartment to let the Sandman take over. Sleep seemed overdue and thus most welcome.

Something Furry, Perhaps

The radio played, "Here comes Santa Claus, here comes Santa Claus…" while Lee waited for the traffic light to turn green. His sleepy eyes may have closed longer than they should have. Had he dozed for a moment? Without warning, Lee became aware of the fat farm nominee standing in front of the Bel Air. As Lee eased up in the seat, he noticed the stranger's eyes reflecting a star-like sparkle from the car's headlights. Lee immediately realized that he was wearing a clean and perfectly pressed Santa Claus costume with boots and buckles brilliantly shined. The charcoaled cap that had been perched on the old man's head with the end resembling a flamed-out marshmallow, had been replaced with a new holiday style cap… one of beauty with rich red and white velvet fabric that was paled only by the brilliance of the impersonator's long silver beard.

The man approached the passenger side door and, without invitation, simply climbed in again. The once overly stuffed canvas sack was now obviously empty and Lee watched as he took time to neatly fold and gently place it on the seat between them.

"Don't need a ride this time, thanks," he said. "Just want to visit a minute and maybe warm myself some before I head home."

"That is really fine," Lee thought to himself. "Here I am tripping around with a self-proclaimed astronaut that doubles as Santa Claus! And how did the rest of you spend your pre-dawn Christmas?"

"Everybody else is probably sleeping like babies," the odd guy answered Lee's thoughts out loud.

Lee glanced around the abandoned streets to see if anyone was witnessing this momentous occasion.

"Thanks again for giving an old duff a lift," Nicky said most sincerely. "What ya gonna do for Christmas?"

Lee found himself uncomfortable with being placed on the spot. "Nothing really," the lad retorted. "I'm not all that into Christmas."

Nicky took a long soft look at Lee and smiled. "I know." Pointing in the direction of the Car Corral (quality used car lot), he went on. "Take it over there and park it. I have someth'n to show ya."

Behind the front row of previously owned transportation, Lee saw something move -- something furry, perhaps; actually, *several* furry somethings. As they drew closer, Lee found himself awestruck for he was to behold a herd of rather large reindeer. "Man!" the lad thought out loud. "You go all out!"

A large candy-apple red sleigh trimmed in gold was attached to the deer with a patent leather harness and reins to match. Lee found himself in total bewilderment as he unconsciously removed himself from the Chevy and approached the tricked-out sled. The young man reached down and drew his fingers gently across the diamond tuck red-velvet doublewide seat.

"That's my favorite part," Nick commented as he patted himself on the backside. "Even with all my built-in stuffing, I can't get enough of the cushion. Climb in and I'll take you for a spin. Besides, I owe you one."

As unreal as it all seemed, Lee still found himself participating in this ridiculous mirage. Perhaps he was just humoring the old fellow or maybe he was actually curious about how long this experience would last. In any event, the young man sat down and made himself comfortable. The old man wasted no time in following Lee's lead. He swiftly climbed in after Lee and while standing, yelled, "Alright boys, make like a tree and leaf; or better yet, make like a leaf and put me back in my seat." And with a chuckle they were off!

"It Ain't a '57 Chevy, But…"

"What now?" Lee thought to himself as he felt the contraption begin to move. It moved kind of slowly at first, but as it gained speed Lee could have sworn he felt it lift a little. He looked down in total horror and disbelief. Like magic, they were soaring upwards and into the heavens. Lee felt the G-force pressing him sternly into the crushed velvet and he did not like it; not one bit! With panic gripping every nerve he gasped for oxygen and looked in the direction of the ever-fading used-car lot. By then, the vehicles were matchbox size and with a blink of an eye, out of sight!

Lee turned his head around for fear that any slight movement might upset the whole "cart." Nicky, by this time, had eased himself slowly but firmly into the seat next to the young man. "She ain't a '57, but she still gives ya a rush, don't she?"

A rush! With a simultaneous sensation Lee could feel his heart beating in his temples and in his crimped toes at the same time! He did not like the prospects of being a splat on the earth's surface, but he was sure to be just that if he fell from the contraption that did not have seatbelts. They soon climbed above the freezing haze that engulfed the sleeping unaware town. Lee became acutely conscious of the temperature feeling warmer as they broke through a large fluff of a cloud. Still feeling a great struggle from within, he placed his fear and anxieties aside the best that he could and began to marvel at the great view. With symbolic wonder a brilliant star glistened, extending a piercing ray of light that seemed to beckon to them. Beneath it, a shallow glow outlined the mountainous horizon giving a hint that dawn was making an eventual introduction to Christmas Day. It was at that point that Lee could actually detect the curvature of the earth, and what a sensational sight it was.

Giant mountains and deep canyons passed swiftly beneath the two, and only an occasional jingle of a harness bell would break the otherwise complete silence. The reindeer appeared as mere shadows, extending again and again in a never broken rhythmic thrust of their legs.

Nicky, also known as Saint Nick or Santa, as Lee would slowly begin to believe when faced with undeniable evidence to the fact, clasped a large gentle hand around the young man's unexpecting arm and nodded in a northerly direction. A magnificent fairytale sight was unveiled before Lee's very eyes. The soft, yet overwhelming dynamic wonder of the Northern Lights with incredible splendor, shimmered like an undecided river as far as one could see. As the lights passed beneath the sleigh, Lee felt as though they were flying over a foreign planet. The snow-covered earth reflected the deep rich fluorescent lights, an image which made the ground appear translucent from within.

"That's where I live," Santa finally broke the silence. He pointed at a large log cabin with all the windows aglow in the distance. "Normally I would be hospitable and introduce you to the Mrs. but she isn't expecting company and the house is pretty much a total disaster area this time of the year. She would never forgive me," he concluded and pulled snugly on the right rein. "She ain't no Sheila, but she sure has my number," he chuckled.

As the jolly old fellow turned the flying fable of the fourth century around, Lee had the feeling that they were heading back towards civilization. By now, he was relaxed and able to enjoy the awe-inspiring experience. As he let himself be taken in, an overwhelming feeling of peace and wellbeing began to spill into his soul.

Lee Awoke With a Start

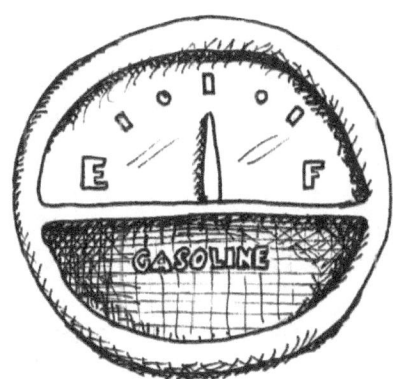

Suddenly, the rhythmic torque of the massive engine ceased and Lee awoke. Stardust's engine had stopped running. Free now from competition from the idle roar of the motor, the Beach Boy's "Round, Round, I Get Around," blared from the radio. Lee's chariot was out of gas. He glanced at his watch and discovered that he had apparently been asleep at the wheel for over 20 minutes. He looked up at the traffic light, which once again cycled to red as if to taunt.

"Oh," the young man said out loud. As the realization sunk in, he became instantly disappointed. The adventure he had just experienced had only been a brief but completely stimulating dream. Lee found himself staring at the gas gauge as if such concentration might make a difference, but the unforgiving needle persisted on "E" being its final resting place. Lee now desperately missed the tremendous joy he felt when he actually thought he was traveling at Mach speed in Santa's mode of elaborate transportation. He wanted to go on believing that Santa and all his magic did exist. He found himself depressed by the prospects of reality and somewhat regretful of the dream all together.

Lee knew better, but, declaring himself a part of the human race and thus subject to human fallacies, he impulsively reached down for the ignition key. If necessary he would will the beast to start! While he did so, he pondered the hopeful prospect that the adventure could have been true.

Stardust sputtered, coughed, and then fired on all eight cylinders. Lee's weary eyes focused on the gas gauge with its needle now resting even further below empty. Knowing he had but only a few precious seconds at best to travel several blocks, he began to release the clutch. His eyes once again fell upon the historically accurate gauge. Somehow the needle seemed to lift a little, lending false hope to his already concrete doubts. At a snail's pace, the needle continued to rise. Lee cocked his head and watched in amazement as it rose past an eighth, then a fourth, finally settling on one half. If the engine hadn't kept running, Lee's mentality would not have conceded to such a phenomenon.

The light finally changed to the long-anticipated color of jade and Lee drove utterly confused to his apartment, all the while struggling with the uncertainty of what was reality and what was a dream. Without further burdening himself with the confusion of the gas gauge he parked the car, entered the boarding house and went upstairs to his modest dwelling. Eventually, he decided to simply give in to mental exhaustion and go to bed. Lee looked forward to crawling under the refuge of his favorite quilt, even though he knew that the prospects of sleeping could include the risk of having another misleading dream.

Extra Colossal Junior Construction Set

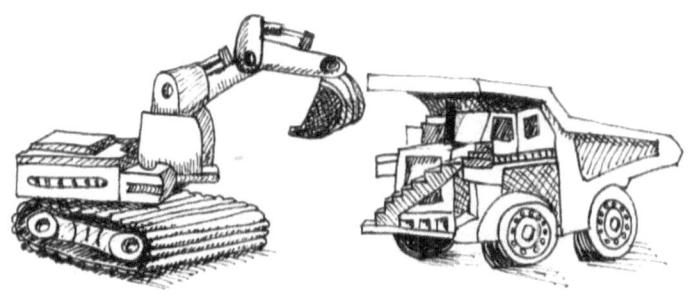

The morning sunshine penetrated its warmth through Lee's window and its brilliance concentrated upon his unprepared face. He rolled half over and, with one eye open, attempted to read the digital numbers of the electric rooster. It was 10:10 and he could hear the next-door children through the paper-thin walls. The monstrous sounds of miniature heavy construction equipment propelled by D-cell batteries reverberated down the hallway and throughout the boarding house. A strange sensation came over Lee as he actually felt such vibration creeping up from the floor, through the bed posts and into the bed's box springs. Two-year-old Liam had most definitely become the Christmas Day recipient of the "Extra Colossal Junior Construction Set" containing bulldozer, excavator, dump trucks, and a front-end loader. All made of long-lasting steel, which is guaranteed stronger than the toughest interior latex; a warranty which Lee was sure Liam was currently testing the limits. Furthermore, to enhance the little one's construction experience, an audio CD conveniently, if not accurately, projected each component's engine, revving at its greatest respective RPM!

But that was not all! Even over the sound of "manly" fabrication in progress, Lee detected the non-relatable cry of, "Go" and the apparent sound of Beyblades striking the surface of a battle colosseum and bumping into each other to see who is dominant. That could only mean that seven-year-old Peyson also struck gold on Santa's wish list.

Conceding his rest, Lee quickly lifted his weary existence from the comfort of the bed and, after a long hot shower and a shave, proceeded to place himself in the confines of a suit that he had not extracted from the innermost depths of the closet for several years. He studied his reflection in the mirror. There, looking back at Lee was a face with a warm smile and blue eyes that seemed to radiate light as if in anticipation of future success and newly acquired dreams come true. Somehow, he had not only come to terms with any disappointment during the previous night's repose, but he actually felt refreshed and once again, for some unknown reason, exhilarated.

The roundtrip flight with Santa Claus may have only been a fantastic dream, but the spark, which was left by such a vivid image, influenced Lee greatly. With sudden expectancy, he felt a surging power from within; a power to make a difference, not only in his own life, but for others as well. Yes, a power so great that he even considered going to church; a structure that hadn't undergone Lee's presence in quite some time. Not fearing the possibilities of structural collapse of such an institution, or even the end of civilization as we know it, Lee rushed down the stairs and leaped into his car.

Santa's Calling Card

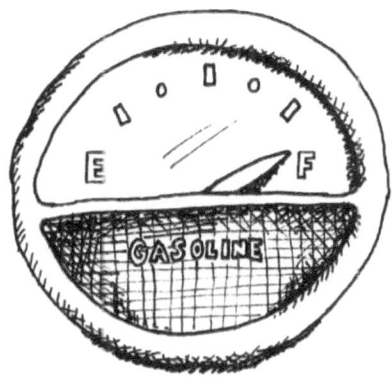

    After Lee climbed into the beautiful vintage model and started its cold hesitant engine, he realized that this automobile, as great as it was, was merely an extension of his passion and a symbol of an era long past. The tremendous combination of rubber, wiring, and steel was, nevertheless, only a car. Lee felt a change from within, and he knew that he would no longer hinge his sense of self-worth on inanimate objects, impressive as they may be. Now, for the first time since he first owned it; *it no longer possessed him*. It no longer represented his identity.

    As suddenly as he made such a distinction, his attention was diverted. Out of the corner of his eye he saw something that did not belong to him. There, on the seat next to him, was the toy sack from his dream... the sack that belonged to Santa Claus. With skeptical hesitancy, Lee picked it up and rolled the fabric between his thumb and fingers. As he slowly brought the cloth sack to his nose, he detected the slight odor of singed hair that was impregnated in the inner weaving of the canvas. The odor suddenly brought Lee's senses forth and, with haste, Lee redirected his attention to the instrument panel. The orange needle of the fuel gauge incredibly rose again. Climbing from a half, then to three quarters, not stopping until the gas tank was full; which once again forced him to consider the validity of the previous evening's involvements.

Thanksgiving

Although Lee arrived late, the church was not as crowded as he had anticipated. As usual, only the front pews were available and the young man felt uncomfortable and a bit conspicuous as he made his way down the center aisle. Out of his peripheral he detected parishioners scooting over as if to make room so that he would not have to sit alone. The thought was appealing to him and he decided to accept the impromptu invitation. As he glanced over, his eyes met with the most beautiful green eyes he had ever seen – those belonging to Sheila. Jasmine was standing in the pew and blurted out a "hi" that was quite audible in the quiet setting. As her little face looked up, Jasmine patted her precious tiny hand on the vacant seat next to her and instructed, "Come sit. Let's talk." Laughter flowed throughout the congregation which seemed to extend appreciation for such innocence.

On the other hand, Isabelle seemed somewhat embarrassed by her little sister's adoring gesture. She just smiled with a shy nervousness and exclaimed in an urgent whisper, "We don't talk in church!"

"I do." Jasmine responded in a regular voice once again.

"I *know*!" Isabelle once again attempted to stifle her sister's enthusiasm.

Jasmine let out a sigh and redirected her attention to Lee. "We'll talk after church."

Lee felt his heart race as he sat down. Sheila must have sensed Lee's uneasiness and she simply reached over and clasped his hand in hers. He was thankful that their first (unofficial) date was in church. It was a venue without expectations, real or perceived; plus, it could set the foundation for their relationship from that point on.

Soon Jordan raised his hands towards Jay and simply said, "Hold you?"

Jay could feel that all eyes were on him so what choice did he have? He lifted the smallest child over Jasmine and "faked" the concept of being comfortable with holding a toddler. Jordan immediately nestled his head on the young man's shoulder as though this had taken place a thousand times before.

Yes, little ones, and older folks too, there is a Santa Claus, and Christmas is for real. It has been seven years since Lee had to endure Nicky's version of "Runaway." He and Sheila are now married and live in a log cabin resembling one in which Mr. and Mrs. Claus might reside. Finding "Slaughterhouse Road" an unacceptable name for such a beautiful path, Sheila decidedly renamed it "Stardust Glade."

Lee and Sheila still have Stardust, not just because she's a boss set of wheels or because of the delightful memories she sparks. Really, it's from a more practical perspective. You see, in the last seven years they have traveled over 80,000 miles and they have yet to put a drop of petrol in the tank.

The Merry Ending

www.ingramcontent.com/pod-product-compliance
Lightning Source LLC
Chambersburg PA
CBHW030241180626
46810CB00008B/3235